P9-DDL-969

Piggy's
PANCAKE
PARLOR

WITHDRAWN
LVC BISHOP LIBRARY

LEBANON VALLEY COLLEGE LIBRARY

· DAVID McPHAIL ·

Piggy's PANCAKE PARLOR

DUTTON CHILDREN'S BOOKS · NEW YORK

For Donna, editor and true believer

Copyright © 2002 by David McPhail
All rights reserved.

LIBRARY OF CONGRESS CATALOGING-IN-PUBLICATION DATA
McPhail, David M.
Piggy's pancake parlor / by David McPhail.—1st ed.
p. cm.
Summary: Piggy and Fox open a restaurant where they serve
the delicious pancakes that Piggy makes by adding a secret ingredient.
ISBN 0-525-45930-8
[1. Pigs—Fiction. 2. Foxes—Fiction. 3. Pancakes, waffles, etc.—Fiction.
4. Restaurants—Fiction. 5. Secrets—Fiction.] I. Title.
PZ7.M2427 Pe 2002
[Fic]—dc21   2001047143

Published in the United States 2002 by Dutton Children's Books,
a division of Penguin Putnam Books for Young Readers
345 Hudson Street, New York, New York 10014
www.penguinputnam.com
Designed by Alyssa Morris and Laurin Lucaire
Printed in China
First Edition
3   5   7   9   10   8   6   4   2

CONTENTS

Piggy

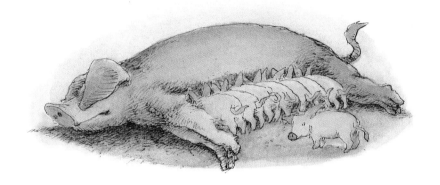

PIGGY GREW UP ON A SMALL FARM just below the hilltop village of West Wee. He was the runt of a large litter of pigs.

The farm was owned by Mr. and Mrs. Farmer Todd, who took Piggy in because he was weak and underfed.

Mrs. Farmer Todd would sit by the fire in her cozy kitchen, holding Piggy in her arms and feeding him from a bottle.

Piggy loved being in the Farmer Todds' kitchen. He loved the warmth of it and the wonderful aromas, for Mrs. Farmer Todd was an excellent cook. She was famous throughout the countryside for her delicious pancakes.

Every day there were pancakes for breakfast. Piggy would get up early to finish his chores so he wouldn't be late.

When Mrs. Farmer Todd hurt her wrist cleaning some rugs and couldn't beat the pancake batter, Piggy did it for her.

"You are a natural-born pancake maker," Mrs. Farmer Todd told him. "Someday I will teach you how to make them."

And a few days later she did just that.

One of Piggy's chores was to gather the eggs from the grumpy chickens and bring them to Mrs. Farmer Todd. As Piggy entered the kitchen on this particular day, Mrs. Farmer Todd was just starting to make the pancakes.

"Come here, Piggy," she said, "and I'll show you how it's done."

She beat three of the eggs into a cup of milk and added a dash of vanilla. Then she sifted three cups of flour into a mixing bowl, along with a tablespoon of baking powder and a pinch of salt.

"Now here's the best part," she said, giggling. She took something from her apron pocket and showed it to Piggy.

"Nutmeg," she whispered as she grated a few grains into the bowl before mixing everything together. "One of the secret ingredients."

"What's the other?" asked Piggy.

"Promise not to tell?"

"Promise," said Piggy.

Mrs. Farmer Todd bent down and whispered into Piggy's ear. "And without that," she told him, "no amount of nutmeg will make a pancake special."

From that day on, Piggy was in charge of making the pancakes.

Fox

LIKE PIGGY, FOX HAD BEEN the smallest of a large litter.

Food was scarce, and for Fox it was even scarcer. His brothers and sisters grabbed most of it for themselves. When he could stand it no longer, he left.

Being on his own was not much better. Food was still hard to come by, and finding a place to sleep was always a challenge.

Things improved for Fox when he took a job in a factory that made lollipops. But when some of the lollipops turned up missing, Fox was falsely accused of stealing them and was fired. So Fox's life of wandering and searching began anew.

Early one morning he found himself walking along the railroad track that ran through the lower pasture of a well-kept farm. The sun had just come up, and Fox, who had not eaten for days, heard the hens in the henhouse clucking.

Fox and Piggy Meet

PIGGY WAS ON HIS WAY to collect the eggs. "Those hens are really noisy this morning," he said to himself.

He opened the henhouse door and stepped inside. When his eyes adjusted to the dim light, Piggy saw what the trouble was.

Standing in the midst of the hens, clutching an armful of eggs, was a scrawny red fox.

"See here," said Piggy. "You've got no right to those eggs. They belong to Mr. and Mrs. Farmer Todd!"

"But I'm starving," said the fox.

Piggy felt sorry for him. "Help me collect the eggs," he told the fox, "and I'll see to it you get a proper meal."

So together Piggy and the fox gathered the eggs and took them to Mrs. Farmer Todd.

"Well, who have we here?" she asked, staring at the starving fox.

"I'm Fox," said the fox.

"The name certainly suits you," said Mrs. Farmer Todd with a chuckle.

"Fox is starving," explained Piggy.

"There's too much food in this world for anyone to go hungry," said Mrs. Farmer Todd. "Why don't you fix your new friend Fox a pile of your pancakes?"

So Piggy did, and when Fox had eaten till he thought he might burst, he told them his story.

"It was awfully crowded at my house," he said. "One fox more or less wouldn't matter much—so I headed out to make my way in the world."

Piggy, who had never been any farther from home than the village, was fascinated by Fox's travels and adventures.

"What I'd like more than anything," Fox said in conclusion, "is to find some work and stay in one place."

Suddenly Piggy had an idea.

He turned to Mrs. Farmer Todd. "Ever since we went to town," he began, "I've been thinking about that vacant building next to the general store—"

"Yes?" said Mrs. Farmer Todd. "What about it?"

"Well," ventured Piggy, "wouldn't it make a good place to go for breakfast?"

"Indeed it would," agreed Mrs. Farmer Todd. "Especially if there were pancakes on the menu!"

"I don't know how to cook anything else," said Piggy, "so it will have to be pancakes."

"You can't run a place like that all by yourself, you know," said Mrs. Farmer Todd. "You'll need some help." She looked at Fox.

"You can count on me," said Fox. "I'd love to help."

That very afternoon, Piggy and Fox went up to the village and took a lease on the vacant building that would become Piggy's Pancake Parlor.

Piggy's Pancake Parlor

EARLY THE NEXT MORNING, Piggy and Fox went to work. Because the building had once been a restaurant, there was plenty to work with. First they gave the place a thorough cleaning. They swept, they scrubbed, and they hauled tons of trash to the dump. They restored the counter and the booths. They repaired the grill and got the refrigerator working. They gave everything a fresh coat of paint.

Then they fixed up a little apartment on the second floor.

It took a lot of hard work to get Piggy's Pancake Parlor up and going. But Piggy and Fox were young and strong, and the hard work agreed with them.

And while Piggy was laying tracks for his model train on a shelf high up on the wall, Fox carved a sign and hung it over the front door.

Mrs. Farmer Todd delivered a wagonload of dishes, cups, bowls, and silverware that she had collected over the years. "I always knew these would come in handy," she told Piggy and Fox.

Finally the day of the Grand Opening arrived. Piggy had been so excited the night before that he hardly slept. And he was worried, too. "What if nobody shows up?" he said to Fox.

But there was no need to worry. When they opened the door to Piggy's Pancake Parlor, a crowd of people was already waiting.

Piggy made the pancakes, and Fox did just about everything else. He served the pancakes, wiped the tables and the counter, and washed all the dirty dishes.

Word spread about Piggy's delicious pancakes. Through-out the day people continued to come.

By closing time, both Piggy and Fox were tired but happy. They locked the door, turned off the lights, and wearily climbed the stairs to their little apartment above the pancake parlor.

They played a game of checkers and read the newspapers before crawling into bed.

"Good night, Fox," said Piggy.

"Good night, Piggy," said Fox. "Pleasant dreams."

One Gruff Customer

PIGGY'S PANCAKE PARLOR SOON BECAME a huge success. People came from all over to savor Piggy's pancakes. Everyone seemed happy to be there—everyone except Mr. Gruff. Mr. Gruff was always grumbling.

"Where are my pancakes?" he would growl. "What's taking so long?"

And even when his pancakes were placed in front of him, Mr. Gruff still complained. The pancakes were too thin or too thick or too small or too big.

And that wasn't all that Mr. Gruff complained about.

The coffee was cold.

The juice wasn't.

All Mr. Gruff's complaining angered Fox and disturbed the other customers, but Piggy just seemed to take it in stride, never letting it bother him.

"I can't stand any more of Mr. Gruff's complaining," Fox said to Piggy one night as they were getting ready for bed. "Next time he complains, I'm going to tell him to leave."

"Let me handle it, Fox," said Piggy.

Sure enough, the next morning Mr. Gruff was there, complaining as usual.

"There's a crumb on the counter!" he howled.

Piggy dropped his spatula and came over to look at the offending morsel.

"There *is* a crumb on the counter!" he cried. "How awful!" He fell to the floor and pounded it with his fists. "How could I be so careless?" Piggy moaned. "A crumb! A crumb! A crumb on the counter! Can you ever forgive me?"

Suddenly Mr. Gruff felt very uncomfortable. He got down on the floor beside Piggy and put his arm around Piggy's shoulders.

"Please stop," he pleaded. "It's only one little crumb. Don't worry about it."

Immediately Piggy got up off the floor and went back to making pancakes.

And Mr. Gruff never complained again.

Piggy Feeds the Children

ONE MORNING WHEN PIGGY WOKE UP, it was raining. By the time he opened the Pancake Parlor, it was really pouring. The wind was blowing hard, driving the rain against the windows.

None of this kept any of Piggy's regular customers away, and the talk at the counter was even livelier than usual. Bad weather will do that.

It was close to noon when the door suddenly burst open, and Wilma Root, the school-bus driver, staggered in.

"The roads are flooded," she cried. "I've got a busload of hungry kids and no way to get them home! What am I going to do?"

"Why, bring them in, of course," said Piggy. "I have yet to meet the child who doesn't like pancakes."

By the time Wilma returned, leading a long line of children, Piggy was already flipping their pancakes.

Fox entertained them with his juggling routines while Piggy cooked. Then, when the children were finished eating, they took turns at the controls of Piggy's electric train.

The children loved being at Piggy's Pancake Parlor. It was the best "field trip" they'd been on all year. Everyone was having so much fun no one noticed that the rain had stopped and the sun had come out.

"Time to go!" Wilma called. "Your folks will be waiting."

The children thanked Piggy and Fox and said good-bye.

"That was fun," said Fox to Piggy as they were closing.

"It was," agreed Piggy, "but I sure am tired."

Both Piggy and Fox slept soundly that night, though Piggy's dreams were often interrupted by cries of "MORE PANCAKES, please."

The Train

W‍HEN P‍IGGY WAS A CHILD, his favorite toy was his electric train. He played with it by the hour, watching it go around and around.

Now the train chugged along on a shelf high up near the ceiling of Piggy's Pancake Parlor.

Fox was fascinated by the train. When things weren't too busy, he sat at the controls, making it go faster or slower, or stopping it and calling: "All aboard for Kansas!"

"Piggy," said Fox one day. "I have an idea!"

"And what would that be?" asked Piggy.

"Let's use the train to deliver pancakes!" Fox replied.

Piggy liked the idea. So that evening, after closing, they lay an oval of track from the griddle to the counter, then along the counter and over to the sink, and finally, from the sink back to the griddle.

Piggy would balance the plates of pancakes on the train, and the train would deliver them to the customers. When the customers were finished eating, the train would take the dirty dishes to the sink. Fox would sit at the controls and make sure everything worked all right.

The next morning, when Caleb Johnson sat down at his usual seat to await his usual order, he was surprised to see a train pull up with a plate of pancakes on it.

"Banana pancakes for Caleb Johnson," he heard Fox's voice calling.

Caleb picked up the plate, and the train whizzed away. If he wanted more syrup or another glass of juice, the train brought it to him. And when he was finished eating, the train took his plate away. Amazing, thought Caleb.

The new pancake-delivery system was a success, but there was so much for the train to do that sometimes it couldn't keep up. So Fox made the train go a little faster, and a little faster still.

Then disaster struck.

The train had just left the griddle with a full load of pancakes. It was heading toward the counter.

"It's going too fast, Fox," warned Piggy.

But it was too late.

The train jumped the track and went careening along the counter, crashing into plates and mugs and spilling pancakes everywhere.

What a mess!

The next day, the train was back on the high shelf where it belonged.

The Stranger

ONE DAY A STRANGER VISITED Piggy's Pancake Parlor. He wore a suit and tie and carried a briefcase. Very few of Piggy's customers ever wore a suit and tie, and Piggy had never seen any of them carrying a briefcase.

The stranger sat down on a stool and placed his briefcase on the counter.

"Are you Piggy?" he asked.

"That's me," said Piggy. "Would you like some pancakes?"

"Actually, I'd like the secret ingredient," said the stranger as he opened his briefcase and turned it toward Piggy. "I've been sent to buy it."

Piggy looked at the briefcase. It was full of money—lots of money. More money than Piggy had ever imagined.

"I can't tell you what the secret ingredient is," Piggy said. "I promised I wouldn't, and a promise is a promise."

"Look again," urged the stranger. "Think of all the things you could do with this money."

Piggy did. He could make things easier for Mr. and Mrs. Farmer Todd, who were getting on in years and still worked much too hard. And he'd always wanted to travel. He thought about all the places he could go. . . .

Piggy reached out and closed the briefcase.

"I can't tell you what the secret ingredient is," he said, "but I can cook you some pancakes."

And he did.

Revealed

"WAKE UP, FOX," SAID PIGGY early one morning. "I have something important to tell you. I've talked it over with Mrs. Farmer Todd, and we agree that the time has come for you to learn how to make the pancakes."

Fox was excited. He'd heard over and over again how it was the famous "secret ingredient" that made Piggy's pancakes so delicious. And now he was going to find out what it was.

Piggy set out the pancake ingredients and showed Fox how to mix the batter.

"Thirty-seven strokes," said Piggy. "No more, no less."

When Fox had done that, Piggy took a small bottle out of his pocket. He turned the bottle upside down and tapped it once, twice. A fine golden powder drifted down onto the batter.

"Nutmeg," whispered Piggy.

"Is that the secret ingredient?" asked Fox.

"That," said Piggy . . .

"... and a little bit of love."

LEBANON VALLEY COLLEGE LIBRARY

Lebanon Valley College
Bishop Library
Annville, PA 17003

GAYLORD RG